Soda Shop Surprise

Stephanie St. Pierre

D1411748

PRICE STERN SLOAN
Los Angeles

For Scott, Elizabeth and Michael
with hugs and kisses

Published by Price Stern Sloan, Inc.
11150 Olympic Boulevard, Suite 650
Los Angeles, California 90064
ISBN: 0-8431-2919-0
Printed in the United States of America
10 9 8 7 6 5 4 3 2 1

Contents

Worries

It was raining. Barbie jumped out of her '57 Chevy and quickly opened her umbrella.

"Midge, where are you?" she said out loud. Barbie was standing in front of a small shop. The windows were covered with white paper. The door was locked. Barbie looked at her watch. "That girl is <u>always</u> late," she said.

"Barbie!" It was Midge. She was running through the rain. Her umbrella had turned inside-out, and she was dripping wet. "I'm sorry I'm late," Midge said. "Hurry, come in." She unlocked the door and threw it open. Barbie stepped inside. Suddenly she noticed that Midge was crying.

"Midge, what's wrong?" Barbie asked.

"I'm so glad you're here, Barbie," Midge said. "I've had the most terrible day."

"Let's get out of these wet coats," said Barbie. "Then tell me all about it."

"Take a good look around," said Midge. "My dream, my Super Soda Shop, this is it."

"Um, well," said Barbie. "It needs a little work." She looked around at the bare walls. Old gray paint was peeling off them. The floor was a mess too. But at the far end of the shop, one wall was covered by a huge old-fashioned mirror. "The mirror is great," said Barbie. Barbie noticed a grill, a freezer and a refrigerator back near the mirror.

"I know," said Midge. "It's the one thing that doesn't need fixing up." Midge sniffed. "But it doesn't make any difference now."

"Oh, don't worry," Barbie said. "A little paint will turn this place around."

"It's not that," said Midge. "I found out this afternoon that I can't borrow money from the bank. Without it, I won't open in time for the city's centennial celebration."

"So open a little later," said Barbie.

"It's not that easy," said Midge. She sighed. "I don't have enough money to buy all the supplies I still need, or pay waiters. I had to call the painters and tell them not to come." Midge sat down on the floor. She rested her chin on her hands. "This is the worst day of my life." It was quiet for a while.

"It's not like you to just give up," said Barbie. "I'm sure there's a way to get things together in time for your grand opening."

"Yesterday I was upset because there wasn't going to be time to make a float for the parade," said Midge. "Now I can't have a shop at all."

"How much time do we have and what do we have to do?" Barbie said. She wasn't going to let her friend give up.

"We have one week," said Midge.

"A whole week?" Barbie said. "That's lots of time! Look, I'll help out. You know Ken and

Christie and Steven will too. I'm sure we can get this place painted and set up in no time." Midge looked a little brighter.

"Would you do that for me?" she asked.

"What are friends for?" said Barbie. She sat down next to her friend. "And I bet you could get Skipper and some of her friends to wait tables for free if you let them keep any tips they make and give them free meals."

"Do you think they would do it?" The sparkle was coming back into Midge's eyes. "I guess I could make do without some of the fancy things I was going to use, like the special ice cream dishes," said Midge. "I could save a lot of money by using paper cups and plates for the first month or two."

"That's the spirit!" said Barbie.

"We'd better get to work then," said Midge. "We don't have time for anything to go wrong. Everything has to go just perfectly."

"What could go wrong?" said Barbie.

2

Friends to the Rescue

"Ken should be here any minute," said Barbie. "I called everybody and they're happy to help out."

"Wonderful!" said Midge. She gave Barbie a big hug. "Thank you so much."

Soon the girls were busy scraping all the yucky old paint away. When Ken arrived, Midge put him to work carrying away all the junk that had been left behind by the last renter. It was hard work.

"Ugh," said Midge. "I'm getting tired. And I'm so dusty." She had little chips of paint all over her.

"Me too," said Barbie. "And thirsty." She sat on a step stool to rest. "How about a soda?"

"Great idea," said Midge. "But the soda hasn't been delivered yet."

Barbie laughed. "Some soda shop this is!"

"I'm ready for a break too," Ken said. "I'll go out and get us some sandwiches."

"Hurrah!" said Midge and Barbie.

"I'll be back as soon as I can," Ken said. The girls cleared a space in the middle of the room and sat on the floor.

"I hope you plan to give your customers a nicer place to sit," said Barbie.

"Oh, wait till you see!" said Midge. "I've ordered these great chairs. They look almost like ice cream cones. So do the tables."

"They sound really cool," said Barbie.

"I thought I'd put the soda counter in front of the mirror," said Midge. "With tall pink stools. It's going to be great." But Midge looked worried.

"What's wrong?" Barbie asked.

"Everything is happening so fast," said Midge. "I'm trying not to worry too much. If you hadn't offered to help this would all be over and done with. Now I still have a chance, but—"

"It's still a little scary, right?" said Barbie.

"Yeah," Midge said. "I'll never have a chance like this again. At least not for a long time. I want everything to work out."

"It will," said Barbie. "We'll make sure it does."

"Did you hear something?" said Midge. She got up from the table and walked toward the back of the store. She stood very still, listening.

"What?" asked Barbie.

"Listen," said Midge. "I hear a...drip." Barbie walked to where Midge was standing. Drip. Drip. Drip.

"I hear it too," said Barbie.

"Oh, no," said Midge. "I have a terrible feeling about this."

"Don't panic," said Barbie. "Maybe it's just the rain." She walked to the storeroom and opened the door. Slowly but steadily water was dripping from the ceiling.

"On the other hand..." Barbie said.

"A leaky roof!" cried Midge. "What am I going

to do?" Just then Ken came back with lunch.

"Boy, is it raining hard out there," he said. "Food's here," he called to the girls.

"We have kind of a problem," said Barbie. Ken came to see what was going on.

"I'll get a bucket," said Ken. "After the rain stops we'll check the roof. It's probably just a little thing." When they finished lunch they got back to work on the walls. Soon all the old paint was scraped away.

"Let's clean up the floor and call it a day," said Barbie. "I'm tired."

"Okay," said Midge. The shop looked much better than it had. "Thank you guys so much. "I'm sorry to be such a worrier."

Ken smiled. "Let's all go home and get some rest. We've got a busy day tomorrow."

"You can say that," said Midge. She looked back at the shop one last time. Then she flipped off the lights and they were out the door.

3

Wet Paint

In the morning Barbie dressed in a pair of old coveralls. She put on a baseball cap, laced up her sneakers and hurried to meet her friends at the Super Soda Shop.

"Hi, Barbie!" Christie and Steven waved from the doorway of the shop. They were waiting for Midge. Ken was there too.

"Where's Midge?" asked Barbie.

"She brought the wrong keys," said Christie. "She had to go back home."

"Poor Midge," said Barbie. "She's so nervous about everything. We've got to help her calm down."

"Here I am!" called Midge. She came running with her keys jingling in front of her. Everyone laughed. "Sorry, guys," she said. "I'll try to keep from being crazy today."

"Just let us in there so we can get to work," said Christie. Finally the door opened and the friends went inside. Midge hurried to the storeroom to check the leak.

"It stopped," she said happily.

"See," said Barbie, "I told you it wasn't such a big deal."

"I'll go fix the roof," said Ken. Christie, Steven, Barbie and Midge set to work painting. The walls were going to be lemon yellow with strawberry pink and mint green trim. There was also a sign to go over the door outside.

"Who's good at letters?" Midge asked. Christie offered to paint the sign. "Be sure the letters aren't crooked," teased Midge.

"Somebody give her a paintbrush and put her in front of a wall," said Christie. "She's driving me nuts." Barbie and Steven pulled Midge over to the wall they were painting.

"Now get to work," joked Barbie. They

turned the radio on to their favorite station. Everyone was dancing and painting and singing. It was really a lot of fun. The shop started to look really neat.

"Okay," Ken said. He had just come back inside. "The roof is all fixed. And you've got your first delivery."

"Delivery?" Midge ran to the door and looked out at the street. "It's the ice cream. This is so exciting!" She ran out to the truck that was being unloaded. Barbie and the others followed. Everyone helped to unload the rest of the ice cream and carry it to the back of the shop near the freezer.

"Uh, oh," said Barbie. She was looking into the freezer. "It's a mess. But don't worry. I'll clean it."

"What if the ice cream melts?" asked Midge.

"It won't take that long," said Barbie. She wanted to think of a way to keep her friend from worrying so much. Suddenly she had an idea.

"Hey, how about giving away free ice cream samples?" said Barbie. "Take one or two of these cartons. Set up a table out front. It will be a good way to let people know you'll be opening up next week."

"That's a great idea!" said Midge.

"I'm almost finished with the sign for outside," said Christie. "We can prop it up in front of the table."

"The shelves are done," said Midge. "But what about the painting?"

"You give out free ice cream samples," said Ken. "The rest of us will keep painting."

Everyone got back to work. Midge was happy and excited. She soon had the table set up. Then she came back for the ice cream. She took two big cartons. Melted ice cream on the outside of the containers dripped down to the floor in a sticky puddle.

"Yuck, what a mess," said Barbie.

"Don't worry," said Midge. "I'll clean it up in a minute."

"Can somebody hand me a can of mint green paint?" asked Ken. He was standing at the top of a tall ladder.

"Here you go," said Barbie.

"Thanks," said Ken. He bent toward Barbie with a gleam in his eye. "Wait," he said. Barbie looked up again and Ken quickly dabbed the tip of her nose with his paint brush.

"Ken!" cried Barbie. "I'll get you for that." Barbie climbed down the ladder and got her own paint brush.

"Be careful, you two," said Christie. "Don't goof around on the ladder."

"Look what he did," said Barbie. She pointed to her green nose. Christie laughed. Ken was laughing too. Barbie couldn't keep from giggling.

"It isn't funny," she said. She tried to stop

laughing. She walked to the mirror. She really did look silly. "Just you wait, Ken," Barbie said. She was about to wipe the paint off her nose when Midge burst into the shop.

"I'm running out of cups," she said. She hurried across the floor. "And I need more spoo...whoa!" Midge slipped in the ice cream mess and went flying. As she fell to the floor, she knocked over a heavy ladder. It fell across her leg with a crash.

"Midge," Barbie called. "Are you okay?"

"Ouch!" cried Midge. "Owww! My leg!"

4

A Bad Break

"Poor Midge," said Barbie. Everyone was trying to help. Ken carefully picked up the ladder. Midge moaned.

"This looks pretty serious," said Barbie.

"I can't believe it," said Midge. "I think my leg might be broken!" She had tears in her eyes but she was trying hard not to cry.

"Oh, no," said Christie. "Should we call a doctor?"

"No," said Midge. "Just take me to the hospital." Ken and Steven helped Midge up. She couldn't stand on her hurt leg.

"Let's go," said Barbie. The guys took Midge to Barbie's car. Barbie got a blanket from the trunk and wrapped it around her friend to keep her warm.

"Don't worry," said Barbie. "We'll be there in a few minutes."

"This is terrible," said Midge. "What will happen to my shop?"

"Let's worry about <u>you</u> for now," said Barbie.

Soon they reached the hospital. Barbie waited for a long time while Midge had X-rays. Finally a nurse told Barbie that Midge did have a broken leg.

"She'll have to stay here for a few days," said the nurse. "Do you want to go to her room with her?"

"Yes," said Barbie. The nurse took Barbie to her friend. Midge was sitting in a wheelchair. The nurse wheeled her to a quiet room.

"Do you want to be the first to sign my cast?" Midge said. "The doctor says it's not a serious injury. It should heal just fine."

"That's great," said Barbie.

"But they want me to stay for three days to be sure the bones are set right," said Midge. "I told them I've got the shop, but..." Midge looked miserable.

"Look, it will be fine," said Barbie. "You can tell us everything you need done. When you come out of the hospital, it will all be taken care of."

"I'm not going to let this silly broken leg ruin my dream," said Midge. She looked at Barbie. Suddenly she started to laugh.

"What is it?" Barbie asked. "What's so funny?"

"Your nose!" said Midge. "You've got a green nose."

"I can't believe it," said Barbie. "I sat in that waiting room full of people with a green nose? And no one noticed." It felt good to laugh.

"I don't know what I would have done without your help today, Barbie," said Midge.

"I didn't do anything special," said Barbie. "May I sign your cast now?"

"Okay," said Midge. Barbie took a bright pink marker out of her bag. "This will liven it up a bit," Barbie said. She signed her name in

big letters and then drew a little strawberry ice cream cone next to it. Midge laughed.

"You'd better get back to the shop and tell everybody what happened," said Midge.

"See you tomorrow," said Barbie. "And don't worry." Barbie left smiling, but she was worried herself. Poor Midge. There had to be a way to save her big opening-day plans.

Back at the shop there was a wonderful surprise .

"It's done!" Barbie was amazed. The shop looked beautiful. The painting was finished.

"We wanted it to be ready in case Midge came back," said Christie. "Is she okay?"

"Her leg is broken," said Barbie. "She can't walk on it at all until they know the bones are setting just right. She'll be in the hospital a few days."

"Oh, dear," said Christie.

"What's wrong?" Barbie asked.

"There's more bad news," said Steven.

"Take a look," said Ken. Barbie looked into the freezer Ken was pointing at.

"Oh, no!" she gasped. "What happened?"

"The freezer doesn't work," said Steven.

"We called a repair man," said Christie. "But he said it couldn't be fixed." All the ice cream had melted.

"Why don't we clean up and go back to my house?" said Barbie. "We need to think how we're going to save Midge's opening day. I think we're going to have a long night." Everyone agreed.

Cleaning the freezer was a messy job. But finally it was done. All they needed to do now was wash out their paint brushes.

"Oh, Ken," said Barbie. "Could you come here for a second?" She picked something up and held it behind her back.

"What do you need?" asked Ken.

"Close your eyes," said Barbie with a twinkle in her blue eyes. Ken closed his eyes. Barbie dabbed his nose with pink paint.

"Hey!" he said. Barbie laughed. Ken looked very funny with a pink nose. He was mad for a minute. Then Barbie told the story of her green nose in the hospital.

"Okay," he said. "Very funny. Now let's get going."

"See you back at my place," said Barbie. She and Ken hopped into her car and drove away. Christie and Steven were close behind.

5

The Plan

"All right," said Barbie. They were sitting in her living room, eating pizza. "We have three problems. First, we need to find a freezer that works. Second, we need to replace all that melted ice cream. And third, we don't want Midge to know about it."

"Fourth, we have only a few days," added Christie.

"Fifth," said Steven, "we don't have any money to buy the freezer or the ice cream."

"Hmmm," said Barbie. She thought for a long time. "I have it!" she cried. "I really think I've got a plan that will work."

"Okay, tell us," said Ken.

"Let's have a raffle," said Barbie. "We can raffle off a couple of free parties at the shop."

"How would it work?" asked Christie.

"We sell tickets to people," said Barbie. "If they win, they get to have a big party for free at the Super Soda Shop."

"It's a great prize," said Ken.

"I think people would buy raffle tickets for that," agreed Steven.

"Do you think it would be all right with Midge?" asked Christie. "What if it costs too much to give a party like that?"

"That's one of the things we've got to plan. How much do the tickets have to cost to pay for the ice cream, the freezer and a couple of parties? We don't want this to cost Midge extra money. If it doesn't, she won't mind."

"So we take the money we earn selling the raffle tickets and buy the new freezer and the ice cream," said Ken.

"There's still a problem," said Christie.

"What?" asked Barbie.

"Time," said Christie.

"I know," said Barbie. "But why not start

tonight? We can call people on the phone. If they want a ticket, they can pay us tomorrow."

"Okay," said Ken. "That could work. If we're lucky, we might even sell enough tickets in one night. But how do we keep it a secret from Midge?"

"Do you think she'll hear anything in the hospital?" asked Christie.

"Maybe," said Barbie. "Once we've got the new freezer it doesn't matter if she knows. We just don't want her to worry while she's supposed to be getting over being hurt."

"Maybe we can just distract her," said Ken.

"How?" asked Steven.

"She said something about wanting to build a float for the big parade," said Barbie.

"So?" Ken and Christie and Steven said all at once.

"So, what if we built one?" said Barbie.

"But how could we?" said Steven.

"Aren't we going to be busy enough already?" asked Ken.

"I think I know just the people to call for help," said Barbie. She picked up the phone and called her little sister, Skipper.

"Hi, Sis," Barbie said. "I need your help."

"What for?" asked Skipper.

"How would you and Courtney and Kevin like to build a giant ice cream soda float for the parade next week?"

"Wow," said Skipper. "That sounds really fun!"

"And you can have all the ice cream you want in exchange for the work you do," Barbie said.

"Great," said Skipper. "I'll call Courtney and Kevin right now."

"Fantastic," said Barbie. "Why don't you meet us tomorrow at the Super Soda Shop? See you then." Barbie hung up the phone.

"I'm not sure I understand this plan," said Christie.

"Well," said Barbie. "Midge will be so busy working out the plans for the float with

Skipper and her friends that I don't think she'll notice that we're up to something."

"It's worth a try," said Ken.

"Besides," said Barbie. "Midge really wanted a float for the parade. It will be fun for her. And she'll get to advertise her shop. And she can work out a deal with the kids to help out as waiters, too."

"So let's decide how much the raffle tickets should cost," said Steven. "Then we can start calling people." They had a long, busy night ahead of them. Finally the plans were settled.

"Bye, everyone," said Barbie. Her friends were going home to make lots of phone calls. Barbie sat down and picked up the phone. Before she started trying to sell raffle tickets, there was someone she needed to call. She dialed and listened to the phone ring.

"Hello?" said a sleepy voice.

"Hi," said Barbie. "I just wanted to see how you were feeling."

"I'm okay," said Midge. "Tell me about the Soda Shop."

"Everything is just fine," said Barbie. "They finished the painting and it looks terrific."

"I can't wait to see it," said Midge.

"I'll call you in the morning," said Barbie. "You can tell me then what you need us to do for you tomorrow."

"Thanks again, Barbie," said Midge.

"I'm happy to help," said Barbie. "Take care of your leg."

"Okay," said Midge. "Bye."

"Bye," said Barbie. She hung up the phone. Then she picked it up again. She made her first raffle ticket call.

6

Double Scoop

"How did everyone do?" Barbie asked. Ken, Steven and Christie were sitting on the floor of the Super Soda Shop with Barbie. "I called seventy-four people and they all bought tickets," said Barbie.

"I've got fifty people who want raffle tickets," said Ken.

"I sold sixty-three," said Steven.

"And I sold only thirty," said Christie. "But that's because I had to stop calling people to draw the tickets."

"They look great," said Barbie. Christie had taken a roll of plain tickets and jazzed them up with a glitter pen and hot pink ink.

"What happens now?" asked Steven.

"We have to collect the money and give people their tickets," said Barbie. "And then we should meet back here and see how much we have at the end of the day."

"How many tickets do we need to sell to cover the cost of the freezer and the ice cream?" asked Ken.

"I think we need to sell between three and four hundred tickets," Barbie said.

"Three hundred?" Christie, Steven and Ken gasped.

"That's not as bad as it seems," said Barbie. "We sold more than two hundred just last night!"

"But I called everyone I know," said Ken. "I can't think of anyone else to call."

"I know," Barbie said. "It's going to be harder today, but we can do it. I know we can." The others agreed to try. Just then Skipper and her friends Kevin and Courtney knocked at the shop door.

"Great," said Barbie. "Plan B can now go into action." She got up and let the kids in.

"Hi, everybody," said Skipper. "When do we get started making this crazy float?"

"Right after we visit Midge at the hospital," said Barbie.

"Why?" Skipper asked.

"Because," said Barbie, "you're going to volunteer to make a float for her and then keep her busy thinking about it for the next two days. That way we can get everything else straightened out."

"Okay," said Skipper. Courtney and Kevin agreed too. Ken and Steven left to sell more raffle tickets and collect money for the ones they had sold already. Christie stayed behind in the shop to wait for the deliveries that would be coming.

"I'll get back as soon as I can," Barbie said. "I'm sure Midge has a million things that need to be done today. I'll talk to her first and then let these kids get her busy thinking about that parade float."

"Okay," said Christie. "I'll be here. Let's just hope things work out better today than they did yesterday."

Barbie and the kids left for the hospital. When they got there they found Midge in bed, trying to reach the crutches the nurse had left for her.

"Aren't you supposed to stay in bed?" asked Barbie.

"I'm so glad you're here," said Midge. "I was going to try to get to the phone down the hall to call you."

"Why not call from here?" Barbie asked.

"Oh, the dumb phone isn't working," said Midge. "What's happening at the shop?"

"Nothing right now," said Barbie. "It's just looking beautifully painted and empty."

"But the deliveries!" Midge cried.

"It's okay," Barbie said. "Christie is there waiting. I came to get a list of everything you need us to do today." Midge thought for a moment then got a pencil and paper and began writing.

"That should cover it all," she said. She handed Barbie a long list.

"Whew," Barbie said. There were so many little details. She was amazed that Midge could keep track of it all. "It's as good as done," Barbie said. "Now I have a surprise for you."

"Oh, boy," said Midge. "I love surprises."

"Come on in, guys," called Barbie. Skipper and Courtney and Kevin had been waiting in the hall. Now they came in carrying a big picture of a giant root beer float on wheels.

"Hey, what is all this?" Midge asked.

"Well," said Skipper. "Barbie told me that you wanted a float in the parade but didn't have any time to make one."

"And?" Midge said.

"And we want to build it if you'll let us," said Courtney.

"We even worked out a design for it," said

Kevin, holding the drawing up again.

"This is fantastic," said Midge. "I would love for you to build it. And it looks great. But what if we put something with the name of the shop on it..." Midge reached for the drawing and began sketching with her pencil. Barbie winked at Skipper and they smiled. The plan was going to work.

7

Triple Trouble

The shop was a mess when Barbie got back. Boxes were stacked almost to the ceiling all along one wall. The center of the room was full of parts of chairs and tables.

"Help!" cried Christie. She waved to Barbie from across the room. A delivery man stood next to Christie looking confused.

"He's supposed to bring in the soda counter," said Christie. "But all these boxes are in the way now."

"Well, we'll just have to move them," said Barbie. She managed a smile and started shoving boxes of hot dog buns and paper napkins out of the way.

"When did all this stuff get here?" asked Barbie.

"About five minutes after you guys left," said Christie. "I can't believe it all came at the same time. But I cleaned up a little more in the storeroom. We can unpack and stock the shelves in there."

"Great," said Barbie. Christie and Barbie pulled some boxes to the storeroom and began unpacking the supplies. Soon they heard the sound of hammering and sawing in the other room. Then they heard another sound they weren't expecting.

"Was that a telephone?" asked Barbie.

"I think so," said Christie. The girls followed the sound of the ringing phone until they found it.

"Hello?" said Barbie.

"Hi!" It was Midge. "I forgot to tell you they turned on the phone this morning."

"We were a little surprised to hear the ringing," said Barbie.

"I was wondering if you would have time to give away some free ice cream today, like we did yesterday?" asked Midge.

"I'd love to," said Barbie, "if we had any—"
Barbie had almost given away their secret.

"What?" said Midge. "Of course you do. There's a whole freezer full of ice cream."

"I meant we didn't have any time," said Barbie. "It's so hectic around here."

"Oh, dear," said Midge. "I told my friend at the daycare center that if she and the children came by after their trip to the park, you would hand out free cones to the children."

"Oh," said Barbie. "Of course we can do that." She had a sinking feeling in her stomach. "What time will they be coming?"

"In about an hour," said Midge. "Is something wrong?"

"Oh, no," said Barbie.

"Do you mind if I call later?" said Midge. "It's not as good as being there, but I don't feel so left out."

"Great," said Barbie. "I'll talk to you later." She hung up the phone and ran to Christie in the storeroom.

"What now?" asked Christie.

"We've got to hand out free ice cream cones to the children from the daycare center," Barbie said. "They'll be here in an hour."

"But we don't have any ice cream!" said Christie.

"I know," said Barbie. "I guess I'll have to go out and buy some. At least we have the cones. Can you find them while I'm gone?"

"What next?" Christie wondered.

Barbie hurried to the store. She bought all the ice cream they had. Then she ran back to the Super Soda Shop to get ready. She had barely set up when the children arrived.

"It was so nice of Midge to do this," said Midge's friend Annie. She was the director of the daycare center. The children were having a great time eating their ice cream, running around the shop. They seemed to like hiding behind the big piles of boxes best.

"Yes," said Barbie. "It was nice of Midge."

She couldn't help laughing. She spooned the last of the ice cream into the last paper cup for the last child.

"I hope nobody wants seconds," Christie whispered. Barbie slumped against her friend for a second.

"Things are getting nutty around here," she said. She was worried that the kids were getting too wild. She didn't want anyone to get hurt. "I still need to call about ordering ice cream and the freezer. And I have to sell some more raffle tickets." Just then Ken and Steven came back.

"Did somebody say raffle tickets?" they asked.

"Hi," said Barbie. She was glad to see them. "First, tell us how you did."

"Terrific," said Ken. "We sold all the tickets." Steven held up an envelope full of money.

"Fantastic!" said Barbie. She gave each of them a big hug.

"Yeah," said Steven. "We just sold our last two tickets to the daycare ladies."

"Uh, oh," said Barbie. The daycare group waved good-bye as they started walking back to the center. "I hope they don't say anything to Midge."

8

A Bright Idea

"This place looks really neat," said Christie at the end of the day. The tables and chairs were set up around the room. They were yellow and green and pink, just like the walls. Tall stools were lined up in front of the counter.

"It's almost ready for business," said Steven.

"As long as nobody wants ice cream," said Barbie. They had sold enough raffle tickets to buy the new freezer and the ice cream. Unfortunately, Barbie couldn't find anyone to deliver all the ice cream they needed in time for the shop's grand opening in four days.

"Try not to feel too bad," said Ken. "Midge will understand."

"Yeah," said Steven. "She might even be relieved that we can't do everything without her."

"I know," said Barbie. "And the shop can open without it. I just wanted everything to be perfect for Midge. She's worked so hard to get this place."

"It's too bad we can't just make ice cream," said Christie.

"Wait a second," Barbie said. "That's a great idea."

"What?" asked Christie.

"Why don't we make the ice cream?" Barbie answered.

"Because it's crazy," said Ken.

"That's one good reason," said Christie. "We don't have time is another."

"And we don't know how is another," added Steven.

"It's not so hard," said Barbie. "All we need is one of those big ice cream makers. I bet we have enough money left from the raffle to buy one."

"I bet that would be a big surprise for Midge," said Ken.

"It would be fun," said Christie. "And everything else does seem to be taken care of."

"Did we agree on making the ice cream?" Barbie asked.

"Hurray for homemade ice cream!" They shouted. Skipper came in while they were laughing and singing hurray for ice cream.

"What's going on in here?" she asked. "Has everybody gone crazy?"

"No," laughed Barbie. "I think we're all just very tired."

"Me too," said Skipper. "We worked all day on the float. Do you want to come see it?"

"Sure," said Barbie. The others agreed.

"I think it's time to close up shop here anyway," said Ken. "Especially if we're coming back tomorrow morning to learn how to make ice cream."

"Gee, that sounds like fun," said Skipper.

"Fun or not, it's the only way the Super Soda Shop is going to have ice cream on opening day," said Barbie. "But I'm too tired to worry about that anymore tonight. Let's go see the float."

The kids had started building the float in the parking lot behind the shop. Kevin's father had donated a small tractor for the base of it.

"We have a little more work to do on the frame," said Skipper. "But can you tell what it's supposed to be?"

"It does look a little like a root beer float," said Barbie. So far the float was just a tall wire frame fastened over the tractor.

"Tomorrow we'll start putting on the papier-mâché," said Courtney. "Then you'll see how great it's going to be."

"Midge had so many good ideas," said Kevin. "She's the one who thought of the tractor."

"I wish Midge wasn't stuck in the hospital," said Barbie.

"You know," said Skipper. "I think you worry too much about Midge. She's really fine."

"Yeah," said Courtney. "And she wants to get back to work so badly."

"We're just trying to help out," said Barbie. But she wondered if maybe they weren't helping out too much. Maybe it would be better to tell Midge about the melted ice cream. Maybe they should let Midge decide if she wanted an ice cream maker in her shop or not.

"You know, Skipper might be right," said Barbie. "Midge likes to be in charge. This place is her dream to work out."

"But we're not trying to take her dream away from her," said Christie. "We've been working really hard to try and save it for her." Barbie thought for a minute.

"Hmm," she said. "Maybe we shouldn't be keeping any secrets from her, though."

As Barbie stood thinking, everyone began drifting toward their cars. They were all tired and wanted to go home.

Suddenly they heard the phone ringing back

in the shop.

"It must be Midge," said Barbie. She turned to run inside and get the phone. "Should I tell her about the ice cream?"

"No," said Christie. "Let's surprise her. She'll just worry if she has to think about that empty new freezer."

Barbie ran inside and picked up the phone.

"Hello," Barbie said.

"Barbie, what is happening to my shop?" It was Midge. And she sounded upset.

9

The Mix-Up

"What do you mean?" Barbie asked. If only she had called Midge earlier tonight. If only she had thought about how Midge might really feel about all the things they had decided for her.

"I mean," said Midge, "my friend Annie from the daycare center just called and told me how excited she is about the raffle and the free ice cream party. What is she talking about?"

"Oh, that," said Barbie. "Well, we thought up the raffle to make some money."

"But why?" asked Midge. "Why didn't you talk to me about it?"

"It all started when the freezer broke down," said Barbie.

"The freezer broke down?"

"Yes," said Barbie. "And all the ice cream melted."

"That's terrible," cried Midge.

"We didn't want to upset you," said Barbie. "So…" Barbie told Midge everything. "We thought it might be fun to get an ice cream maker for the store," she said finally.

"Didn't you think I might want to have a say in something like that?" asked Midge.

"Well, yes," said Barbie. "We've been so busy. We've been trying to make things easier for you. I guess we got a little carried away."

"I'll say," said Midge. She sounded mad still.

"I'm really sorry, Midge," said Barbie. "We were only trying to help."

"Oh, I know that," said Midge. "It's just that I'm mad that I'm stuck in this stupid hospital. I want to make the decisions about my own shop. I want to handle all the problems. I <u>want</u> to worry about all that. It's sort of fun."

"Fun," Barbie laughed. "If you say so."

"Anyway," said Midge. "I think you're all great friends. And the raffle was a fantastic idea. And you're even right about the ice cream maker."

"I'm glad you think so," said Barbie.

"But could I pick it out myself?" asked Midge.

"Oh, sure," said Barbie. She felt glad that Midge knew what was happening. The girls said good night and hung up the phone. The rest of the gang was waiting outside.

"So?" Christie asked.

"She heard about the raffle," said Barbie. "And she was pretty mad."

"Oh dear," said Skipper.

"But it worked out all right," said Barbie. "Now let's go home."

The next few days were very busy. Poor Midge wasn't allowed out of the hospital until the day of the grand opening.

"I can't believe they are making me stay here," said Midge. "I don't know what I would have done without you guys to help." She and

Barbie spent a lot of time on the phone going over every last detail.

"I think we've finally figured out how to make the ice cream," said Barbie. "It took about ten tries!"

"How's the float coming?" Midge asked.

"They're putting the finishing touches on it now," said Barbie. "It looks terrific."

As Barbie and Midge were talking, Barbie was pouring stuff into the ice cream maker. Suddenly she noticed Skipper across the room waving at her and calling for her to stop.

"Midge, I've got to go," said Barbie. She hung up the phone and switched on the ice creamer maker.

"Stop!" Skipper cried.

10

A Dream Come True

"What's the matter with you, Skipper?" said Barbie. Christie came running out of the storeroom where she had been working.

"Turn that thing off!" Skipper yelled. "You just poured my white paint into it!"

"Oh my gosh!" Barbie cried. "I thought it was the cream." The girls dumped the paint out into the sink and cleaned the ice cream maker.

"That was close," said Barbie. She wiped her forehead with a painted hand.

"Boy, will I be glad when this place is opened up," said Christie.

"Tomorrow's the big day," said Skipper.

"And as soon as I finish making this next batch of ice cream," said Barbie, "I'm going out to buy a new outfit to wear for the parade.

Midge wants me to ride on the float and wave at everyone."

"You'll have a great time," said Christie.

"I know," said Barbie. "I'm just not sure what to wear with a giant root beer float." Finally the ice cream was made and put safely in the new freezer. The storeroom was full of supplies. The hot dog grill was ready to go.

"Now all we need is Midge," said Barbie. She shut off the lights and the three girls left for the night. In the morning the Super Soda Shop would open.

"I'm so excited," said Midge. It was opening day. "I can't get the key to turn in the lock."

"Let me help," said Barbie. She had picked Midge up at the hospital and brought her straight to the shop. Midge wanted a chance to look at the place before it filled up with the opening day crowd.

"It's wonderful," said Midge. She was so

happy she almost cried. "It's just like I pictured it, only better."

"We really wanted you to be happy with it," said Barbie. "Just because you couldn't do it yourself didn't mean it couldn't be what you'd planned."

"I'd give you a hug," said Midge, "but I'd fall off my crutches!" Barbie leaned over to hug her friend.

"Now I've got to get onto that root beer float before they leave without me," said Barbie. Skipper and Kevin were out back getting the float revved up to go.

"You look beautiful, Barbie," said Skipper. Barbie was wearing a fluffy white gown. It had short puffy white sleeves and a pale pink top. Her long hair was brushed out over her shoulders.

"I thought this dress looked a little like whipped cream," laughed Barbie. "It seemed perfect for today." She climbed onto the float and got into the seat they'd made especially for her to sit in. She waved to Midge. "There's one more surprise for you," Barbie said. "But you have to wait until we come back to get it."

Midge watched the float drive away. She was looking forward to having a little quiet time in her new shop before she opened for business. Soon the float reached the end of the street where the parade had just begun.

"Wow," said Barbie. "Everybody is here." The streets were lined with crowds of smiling, cheering people. They were happy to see Barbie. Some of them waved their glittering raffle tickets as the Super Soda Shop float slowly moved past them.

"I hope Midge likes my surprise," Barbie thought. As much fun as she had in the parade, Barbie was eager to get back to the shop. Finally the parade was over. A small crowd of people followed the float as it drove back to the Super Soda Shop.

Midge laughed as she watched from inside. It was funny to see her best friend floating up the street in a giant ice cream soda.

Suddenly the Super Soda Shop was full of people.

"Ladies and gentleman," said Midge. "Please take a close look at your tickets now!" The sounds of rustling paper, whispers and giggles came from the excited crowd.

"Before I pick the winning ticket out of this bowl..." said Midge. She held up a big round glass bowl full of ticket stubs. The crowd cheered. "I'd like to thank all my friends for helping to make my dreams come true." Midge waved for Barbie, Christie and the others to join her.

"We were happy to help," whispered Barbie. "Now pick the ticket. We can't wait to see who the winner is."

"And the winner is..." Midge pulled out a ticket and held it up. "The Community Hall Daycare Center!"

"Hurray!" cheered the crowd.

"I'm so glad they won," said Barbie.

"What a fun party that will be," Christie added. "Those kids will have such a good time."

After the raffle drawing, the shop opened for business. Every table was taken. Every seat at the counter was full. And there was a line outside of people waiting to come in for a treat.

"I wish I could get out there and run around," said Midge. Until her leg healed she had to spend her time behind the counter.

"We have another little surprise for you," said Barbie.

"I can't believe it," said Midge.

"Close your eyes," Ken said. Midge closed her eyes. She heard some scraping sounds and a heavy thud across the room.

"What are you guys up to now?" she wondered.

"Just wait a second," said Barbie.

"Come on, turn it on," Christie whispered. There was a loud hissing sound and then suddenly the room filled with the rock and roll sound of Barbie and the Beat.

"A jukebox!" cried Midge.

"We had some money left over from the raffle," said Barbie. "We thought this was the perfect opening-day present for you."

"Oh, it is," said Midge. "I just wish I could get up and dance."

"Well, you have to watch," said Barbie. "But I don't. Come on, Ken." Soon Barbie and Ken and Christie and Steven had cleared just enough space near the jukebox to dance. Before long other people joined them.

"This has got to be the most exciting grand opening party I've ever been to," said a customer sitting at the counter.

"And the food is delicious," said another. Midge smiled.

"I've never tasted such good ice cream," Midge heard.

"And I have the greatest friends in the world," thought Midge. After such a wonderful opening day, Midge knew her shop would be a success. She didn't have to worry about losing the place anymore. It was really a dream come true.

Midge looked up and saw Barbie waving at her. She had a big bright smile on her face. Midge smiled too, then called to her friend, "Barbie, you're the best!"